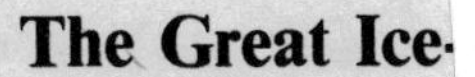

The Great Ice-

Lenny prodded the bag
baton and the bird flew away. Then, slowly and carefully, Lenny moved in and drew back the zip.

The bag was full of money! There must have been a fortune, stuffed to its brim in one-pound and five-pound notes.

Also in Beaver by Hazel Townson

The Barley Sugar Ghosts
The Siege of Cobb Street School
The Vanishing Gran
The Speckled Panic
The Shrieking Face
Haunted Ivy

The Great Ice-cream Crime

Hazel Townson

Illustrated by Philippe Dupasquier

Beaver Books

A Beaver Book
Published by Arrow Books Limited
62-65 Chandos Place, London WC2N 4NW

An imprint of Century Hutchinson Ltd

London Melbourne Sydney Auckland Johannesburg
and agencies throughout the world

First published by Andersen Press 1981
Beaver edition 1983
Reprinted 1983 and 1986

Printed and bound in Great Britain by
Anchor Brendon Ltd, Tiptree, Essex

ISBN 0 09 948640 7

Contents

In memory of my sister-in-law, Cora Shaw,
and for Samantha

1

The dark blue shopping-bag

It was the day the Princess was coming to open the new hospital, and all the schools had been given the morning off to line the route and cheer.

Lenny Hargreaves didn't intend to cheer. He had more important things than royalty to think of. He was going off into the woods by himself to practise his conjuring tricks. One day Lenny intended to be the star performer in the Magic Circle on television.

Lenny knew that the secret of being a good illusionist was secrecy, so he had taken to practising in the woods, where nobody but the birds could see.

Lenny's best friend, Jake Allen, was not magic-minded. He could have joined the act as Lenny's assistant, but had no wish to make a fool of himself. Maybe one day Lenny would really master the Disappearing Jampot and the Floating Aces tricks. In the meantime, Jake would stick to more down-to-earth amusements, such as stamp-collecting, or trying to spot all the Princess's private detectives.

It was a beautiful summer's day. All the children of Cobb Street Primary School – (except, of course, Lenny Hargreaves and a girl called Erica Carr who had chicken-pox) – marched in a crocodile to Redcross Road, which was where the new

hospital stood. The hospital was on a hill, and its front windows had a pleasant view across fields and woods.

The Cobb Street children had been led to a strip of pavement just opposite the hospital's main gates, and now, with their backs to the fields and woods, they packed themselves excitedly into the space right next to their old rivals, St Bernard's Juniors, whom they jostled, booed and taunted. That was fun for a while, but then everyone began to grow hot, thirsty, bored and restless. To make things worse, they could see the ice-cream van in the field behind them, but were not allowed to run off and buy refreshments. The morning threatened to stretch out very long indeed, especially as the Princess was reported to be late. Jake Allen began to wish he had gone off to the woods with Lenny Hargreaves after all, and looked around desperately for a chance of escape.

Meanwhile, Lenny had found his usual spot at the foot of a beech tree in the middle of the woods. There he set up his lightweight, black-draped, folding table, ate half a bar of chocolate, and began:

'Ladies and gentlemen, today you will be privileged to see the Tenfold Trick, or how to finish up with ten times more money than you started with. Here, you will observe, I have a ha'penny. I place it on the table, so, and cover it with this cloth. Now I pass my magic baton over it and say the magic words, "Zin, Zan, Zen, multiply by ten!"'

Lenny whipped away the cloth to reveal two coins instead of one – a ha'penny and a five-penny piece. The ha'penny ought to have disappeared. Ignoring this slight hitch, Lenny continued:

'Now we cover up the five-penny piece with the cloth and try again. Zin, Zan, Zen, multiply by ten!'

Once more Lenny whipped away

MAGIC

the cloth to reveal a fifty-penny piece, only this time he whipped the cloth away so smartly that the fifty-penny piece flew through the air and almost disappeared from sight. Lenny ran after it. It lay in the grass beside a bit of paper which, to Lenny's utter astonishment, turned out to be a five-pound note! Lenny slapped his magic baton down on top of the fiver to stop it from blowing away, and that was when he spotted the dark blue mound half-hidden among the bracken under a nearby tree.

The dark blue mound looked like a shopping-bag, but surely a bulging shopping-bag was a curious thing to find lying among the bracken in a wood? Lenny eyed the bag warily. Perhaps it was a bomb.

Suddenly, a bird, chirruping noisily, alighted on the bag and hopped all the way along the zip to peck at one of the handles.

'Can't be a bomb, then,' Lenny

thought, with a certain amount of disappointment, 'or the bird would have set it off.'

Lenny prodded the bag gently with his magic baton and the bird flew away. Then, slowly and carefully, Lenny moved in and drew back the zip.

The bag was full of money! There must have been a fortune, stuffed to its brim in one-pound and five-pound notes.

Speechlessly, Lenny gazed at his magic baton, then at the bag. At last he selected one of the notes and held it up to the light. There was that metal strip you were supposed to look for, to prove that the money was real. Lenny plunged his hands into the bag, just for the thrill of feeling all that money. What a staggering thing to happen! Could it have anything to do with his magic?

'Zin, Zan, Zen!' he whispered, thinking wildly of all the things that money could buy, from a solid gold bicycle to your own private island stacked with non-melting chocolate bars. But instead of the bag turning into ten bags of money, a shadow loomed behind Lenny, a hand fell heavily on to his shoulder and a voice cried, 'Caught you!'

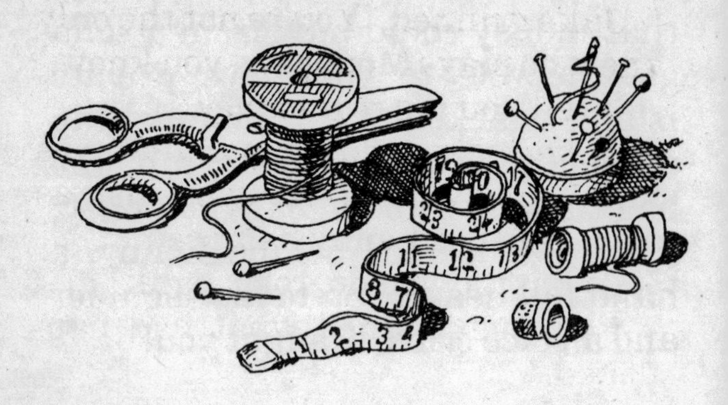

2

The five-star aunt

Lenny Hargreaves lost his balance as he swung round to face his friend, Jake Allen.

'Idiot! You nearly frightened me to death! If you creep up on me like that again I'll have your brains for bike-oil.'

Jake stared at the bag of money.

'Hey, that's good! Is it your Zin-Zan-Whatsit trick?'

'It's not a trick – it's real money. I found it.'

Jake grinned. 'You're not the only one who plays Monopoly, you know.'

'I tell you it's *real money.*'

Jake took a closer look and was finally convinced. He was just as astounded as Lenny had been.

'What did you do, rob a bank?'

Lenny explained what had happened.

'Well, it certainly wasn't your magic. Somebody must have lost it. We'd better take it to the police.'

'Yes, I suppose so,' sighed Lenny, the vision of his chocolate island melting fast.

'There might be a reward,' Jake added hopefully. 'Here, give me one handle and I'll help you carry it.'

In a state of great excitement the two boys set off through the woods with the bag, speculating as to how the money could have been lost.

'Somebody sat down for a rest and left it behind.'

'Must have lost his memory, then.'

'It might have tumbled off the back of a horse.'

'Or fallen out of an aeroplane.'

'No, a helicopter.'

'Or somebody buried it and the rain washed the earth away. Or what if they buried it with a body, and then. . . .'

Their ideas grew wilder and wilder.

They must have walked at least a mile before Lenny suddenly stopped and groaned: 'My magic stuff! I've left it behind!'

Jake sneered disgustedly, but he knew they would have to go back. That equipment meant so much to Lenny. They plodded back in silence, but when they arrived at Lenny's beech tree there was no sign of the folding table and the box of tricks. Lenny couldn't believe it. He rushed around, kicking the bracken aside and scratching himself on the brambles.

'You sure you've got the right tree?'

''Course I'm sure! I've been practising here for weeks. Look, the ground's so soft just here that you can see my footprints anyway.'

Jake studied the ground.

'You've got one foot bigger than the other. Or else there's somebody else's footprints mixed in with yours.'

'You're right! Somebody's been here since we left and pinched my stuff. A big bloke, by the look of it.'

'Maybe you pinched his bag of money.'

'Well, he's not going to get away with my magic stuff. He can't have gone far. Let's see if we can catch him up. There's another big footprint. And one over there.'

The boys began to work their way through the wood once more, but this time in the opposite direction. Instead of coming out at the golf-course end, they would now emerge in the fields across from the new hospital.

'We'll have to be careful no teacher

spots us,' warned Jake, remembering the difficulties of slipping away earlier.

'I've lost track of the footprints now,' said Lenny.

Suddenly he stopped. 'Here, I wonder if all this money has anything to do with the Princess's visit?'

'How do you mean?'

'Well, just suppose you wanted somebody to kidnap the Princess, or shoot her, or something. You'd have to pay them a lot of money.'

'You've been watching too much television,' sneered Jake.

'No, I haven't. In 1974 somebody tried to kidnap Princess Anne and her husband right in the middle of London, so there! Her chauffeur and her private detective got shot, and this man in a taxi who was following behind.' This item of news had made a great sensation at the time, and in fact Lenny's mother had kept the newspaper which had a picture of the shattered royal car.

Jake remembered that this was true. Lenny had even shown him the newspaper once. So now the thought crept into Jake's mind that perhaps Lenny was right. After all, it *was* a lot of money.

Jake sprang into life. 'Come on, then! The sooner we get to the police with this bag, the better.'

The boys began to run out of the woods and across the field towards

Redcross Road, not caring any more whether teachers should see them or not. In fact, all the better if they did. But of course when you want to be spotted, then nobody sees you at all.

The boys had passed no one in the woods, and the first sign of life they saw was Lucci's ice-cream van, parked at the far side of the field behind Redcross Road. The van had a queue, which a man and a woman in white coats were busy serving.

Jake was hot and thirsty. He would have loved an ice-cream, but knew there was no time to stop. They must grab the first policeman they saw – and there he was, standing right on the pavement edge in front of St Bernard's Juniors.

Alas! Jake Allen was from the enemy camp. St Bernard's Juniors wouldn't let him through.

'Get back, Allen!'

'Yeah, stick with your own rotten lot.'

'Give him a kick! Bloomin' cheek, barging in on our patch.'

Jake fought and struggled, but it was no use. He had about as much chance of reaching that policeman as he had of marrying the Princess. He even called out, but the policeman took no notice. Finally, bruised and battered, he withdrew.

Meanwhile, Lenny had spotted something. On the ground underneath Lucci's ice-cream van was a playing-card. Not an ordinary playing-card, but a trick one, with the top left-hand corner showing the four of hearts, and the bottom right-hand corner showing the nine of spades. It was exactly the same as one of the cards in Lenny's box of tricks.

'Hey!' cried Lenny angrily, leaping forward to grab the card.

He ran up to the ice-cream van with it and pushed his way to the front of the queue, meeting much the same opposition as Jake.

'There's a queue in case you hadn't noticed.'

'Get to the back and wait your turn.'

'Who does he think he is?'

But Lenny was oblivious of insult or injury.

'Have you got my magic stuff?' he called out to the ice-cream man. 'I want it back; it's mine!'

The white-coated couple both looked up at once. The man's eyes alighted on the dark blue shopping-bag which Lenny was still holding. A sudden, nasty change came over the man's face. He gave an unintelligible yell, then swung round to the back door of the van.

Sensing danger, Lenny fled. He heard the van door open and the ice-cream man shout again, but he didn't turn to look. Swiftly he caught up Jake and dragged him away round the back of the crowd towards the Cobb Street contingent.

'Quick! We've been spotted!'

cream
Luci's ices

Lenny plunged in among his cronies and Jake followed. Unlike St Bernard's Juniors, the Cobb Street ranks obligingly gave way, and cheered their comrades on. Jake heard a bellow of rage behind him and turned to see a man in a white coat struggling after him. The look on that man's face made Jake feel cold all over.

Just as Jake thought the man was bound to reach out and grab him, a terrific cheer went up from the

crowd. Two police motor-cyclists had appeared, riding sedately down the middle of the road at the head of the Princess's motorcade. The great moment had come!

As the crowd surged forward, so Lenny and Jake spilled forth on to the road. Seizing their chance, they ran like mad to the other side, just in time to avoid being mown down by the motor-cyclists. The ice-cream man was not so lucky. A policeman, leaping in to quell the disturbance, grabbed him before he could dash into the road, and kept him fuming helplessly while the long, slow procession drove by, slowing down even more to take the bend into the hospital grounds.

The cheers were deafening; the excitement was intense. Even the weary teachers began to think the whole thing worth while as the Princess, in a gorgeous peacock-blue outfit, smiled and waved at them.

By the time the procession had passed into the hospital grounds, there was no sign of Jake and Lenny. They had run away down Orbit Street.

'Got to get rid of this bag,' panted Lenny. 'Hide it somewhere, then he daren't kill us till we've told him where it is.'

'*Kill* us?' echoed Jake in horror.

'One consolation, he won't do anything to the Princess either, until he gets his hands on the money. Where can we hide it quick?'

'How about my Aunt Ada's, just round the corner from here?'

Now it was Lenny's turn to follow, as Jake led the way to a neat little house at the end of a row.

'Won't your Aunt Ada be out watching the procession?'

'No, standing about too long makes her back ache. My dad says it runs in the family.'

Jake knocked on the door and a mumbly voice cried, 'Come in!' The two boys obeyed, closing the door thankfully after them.

'Hello, Aunt Ada. It's me and my friend Lenny Hargreaves. Just come to see how you are.'

Aunt Ada mumbled a greeting through a mouthful of pins, for she was dressmaking. She was a pleasant, plump lady with quick fingers and twinkly eyes, and nodded vigorous approval of the boys' visit. At least a three-star aunt, was Lenny's first impression.

'We're not stopping, Auntie. We just wondered if you'd do us a favour.'

'Hungry?' Aunt Ada's pin-stuck grin conveyed that she knew all about boys and the sort of favours they wanted.

'No, it's not that. We want you to look after something for us.'

Jake glanced at Lenny for help, and Lenny nodded encouragingly.

'It's a bag of money. Can we hide it somewhere?'

'Why not? Put it in the spare back bedroom if you like,' said Aunt Ada, stabbing home her last pin.

'We think it's worth about a million pounds. Do you want to look?'

'Not really, dear. I'll take your word for it. I'm trying to get finished before your Uncle Bert comes home for his lunch.'

Aunt Ada stuffed the edge of a pale blue garment under the foot of the sewing-machine and stepped on the starter-button. The machine began to hum, the cloth moved steadily backwards, and Aunt Ada's quick fingers began to pluck away the pins she had just put in so carefully. She was leaning forward, concentrating so hard that she did not even turn as the boys went off upstairs with the dark blue shopping-bag.

Jake looked carefully out of the bedroom window, to make sure the coast was clear. The ice-cream man must never know they had been here. Mind you, if he did find out, he'd have Uncle Bert to contend with, and Uncle Bert had been a well-known local amateur wrestler in his younger days.

Jake had a good look around the bedroom and decided to hide the bag in the bottom of a wardrobe which contained a few old dresses

Aunt Ada no longer wore. They were probably awaiting the next church jumble sale. One of the dresses had fallen from its hanger, so Jake draped it over the shopping-bag as an extra precaution. Then he re-checked that the street was empty and the boys went downstairs.

'Thanks, Auntie. We'll have to be going now.'

'Don't you want some ginger parkin?' cried Aunt Ada in amazement. 'I've only just baked it. I'm surprised you didn't smell it as soon as you came in.'

What a pity, but there really was no time for refreshments. If the Princess was to be saved, the boys must move fast.

'Thanks all the same, Auntie, but we have to go. Don't tell anyone about the money, will you?'

'My lips are sealed,' replied Aunt Ada solemnly. 'Give my love to your mum and dad, then.'

The boys slipped out of the front

door to the accompaniment of the hum of the sewing-machine, and Aunt Ada shouting, 'Whoops!' as her needle ran off the edge of the hem.

'Definitely a five-star aunt!' said Lenny.

3

The shock in the cellar

'Where to now?' asked Lenny.

'Police station, of course. Let them sort it out.'

The boys ran all the way, and when they arrived they found Constable Barlow sitting alone by the telephone, furtively filling in his football coupon. Everyone else was out on procession duty.

'There's going to be an assassination or something,' Lenny blurted out.

'Somebody's after the Princess,' added Jake.

A wary look came into Constable Barlow's eye. He'd had trouble with young lads like this before.

'It's not April the First, you know,' he told them sternly. 'And the police force isn't half as daft as you think it is.'

'It's the ice-cream man,' continued Lenny.

'Well, him and a woman, both strangers, though it still says "Lucci's Ices" on the van.'

'Now, you look here . . .' began Constable Barlow, but he couldn't get another word in. Lenny and Jake were both talking at once.

'I was doing my conjuring in the wood. . . .'

'His fifty pence flew away and landed on a fiver. . . .'

'And then I saw this dark blue shopping-bag with about a million pounds in it. . . .'

'And he hit it with his magic

baton and then we found all these notes. . . .'

'And I thought it was a bomb but it wasn't. . . .'

'And they're real because they've all got metal bits. . . .'

Constable Barlow brought his fist down on the top of the desk with a thump.

'Shut up, the pair of you! That's better! Now, listen to me. We're having a hard enough day as it is, without you kids starting. Do you know what it's like, having a royal visit right through the middle of your patch?'

The Constable went on to describe at length the agonies of such a task.

'But it's *true*!'

'Don't you believe us?'

'We wouldn't make up a story like that.'

'We're trying to help, and I'll bet you'd get promoted or knighted or something if you saved her life.'

Constable Barlow flapped his hands despairingly.

'All right, all right! Go on, then, give us a bit of proof. Let's see this bag of money for a start.'

'We haven't got it. The ice-cream man was chasing us, so we hid it.'

'Hid it where?'

'We can't tell you that. Suppose this room's bugged. . . .'

'Yes, they might be listening in.'

'Oh, give me strength!' prayed Constable Barlow. 'If you two aren't off these premises in ten seconds flat, I'll bundle you into the cells, so help me!' He rushed furiously round the desk, put a hand on each boy's back and swept both lads to the door.

'Go on, get out of it!'

'I don't know why we bother,' grumbled Lenny. 'Nobody ever believes a thing we say.'

He and Jake slunk moodily round the corner – and immediately spotted the ice-cream man again.

He was moving towards them, and saw them at once.

Luckily, the boys were near to a bus stop. Jake ran to flag down the bus that mercifully appeared, and they both jumped on to it.

'Phew! That was close!'

'What if he follows us in a taxi?'

'Well, at least we're drawing him away from the Princess. We're saving her life. How long is she staying at the hospital?'

'At least an hour. Apart from the opening ceremony, she's going round all the wards, chatting to the patients to cheer them up.'

'Right, then we've time to ride as far as the Post Office. We'll go into a call-box and ring up Buckingham Palace.'

'We don't know the number,' Jake pointed out.

'We'll soon find out,' retorted Lenny confidently. He walked straight into the call-box and dialled Directory Enquiries.

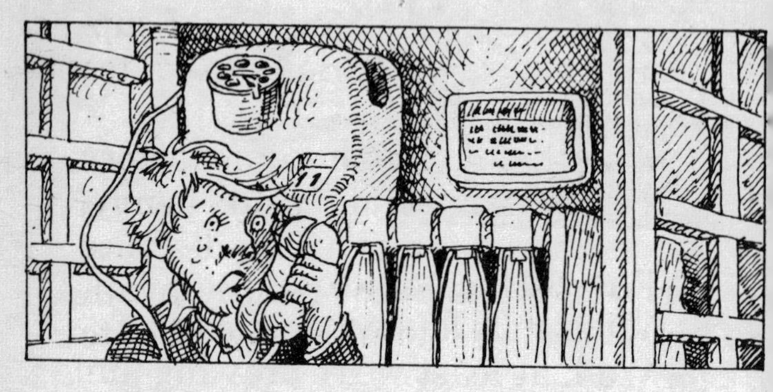

'Please could you give me the number of Buckingham Palace?'

Lenny was quite unprepared for

the fervour with which the operator told him to get off the line or else.

'And I know which phone box you're in, so you needn't think you can vandalise it, either!'

'Crusty old cow!' grumbled Lenny. 'It'll be her fault now if the Princess gets murdered.'

'We could send a telegram to the Queen.'

'I've only five pence left. How about you?'

'Seven pence,' Jake concluded gloomily, having searched every one of his pockets. 'Anyway, I suppose a telegram would take too long.'

'We could go round to the factory and tell your dad,' said Lenny, whose own dad was a long-distance lorry-driver and not readily available. 'Your dad would know what to do.'

'Yeah, that's a good idea. The only thing is, he told me not to hang around the factory any more.

My mum's scared I'll fall in the canal.'

'It's an emergency, in case you'd forgotten.'

'Oh, all right. Come on, then. We'll take the short cut across the Deads.'

The 'Deads' was the children's name for a block of empty houses which were waiting to be pulled down. The trouble was that the Council had run out of money, so nobody was actually working on the job. The houses sat there, dirty and silent, with their doors and windows boarded up and their roofs falling in. Some of the houses even had wooden props to hold them up.

'Gives me the shivers, coming round here,' admitted Jake. 'I'll bet there are rats.'

'Old tramps and squatters, more likely.'

'Squatters? You'd have to be pretty desperate to squat round here.'

BAKER

'I once had a dream that I came down here at night and there was this crippled old hag hunched up in a corner in a long, black cloak, and her face was all twisted sideways. . . .'

'Hey, what's that noise?' Jake had stopped and grabbed Lenny's arm.

Lenny listened. He heard the 'Teddy Bears' Picnic' tune, being played by Lucci's ice-cream van not too far away.

'Quick! Dash into the nearest house!'

'We can't. They're all boarded up.'

It was true. The boys ran along the row like frightened mice in search of a hole, and all the time the sound of the ice-cream van was drawing nearer. Only when they reached the last house did Jake and Lenny see a ray of hope. The boards across one of its glassless windows had been disturbed.

'We could climb in there!' cried Jake at once, and that was exactly what they did, the back half of Lenny disappearing from sight just as Lucci's ice-cream van turned the corner into the street.

It was gloomy inside the house, the only light coming in from the broken boards of the downstairs window. Jake and Lenny stood still for a while, recovering their breath and letting their eyes grow accustomed to the dark.

'Tune's stopped!' whispered Jake.

'I'll bet they're right outside. They'll see where we came in.'

'Come on, then! We'd better go down the cellar.'

Worn stone steps at the back of the house led down into an even darker place which smelled damp and nasty. The boys didn't fancy it much, but it was certainly better than being captured by assassins. There was a door at the top of the steps, and Lenny closed this after him, wondering whether they could find anything to barricade it with. Surely there would be some kind of rubbish in a cellar? Barrels, and stuff like that. He was about to suggest a search when Jake grabbed his arm once more.

'Hear that?' he asked in a croaky whisper. 'There's somebody – or something – over in that corner.'

4

The church jumble sale

When Uncle Bert came home for his lunch, Aunt Ada told him of the boys' visit.

'They were playing some sort of a game,' she said. 'Bank robbers or something, you know what boys are. Always has plenty of imagination, has our Jake. Takes after his mother.'

Uncle Bert grunted, remembering the imaginative patterns on the ties and socks Jake's mother gave at

Christmas. Then he sat down to his hot meal, grumbling at the crowds which had made him late home.

'Don't know why they need a Princess to open a hospital. It's only a matter of cutting a bit of ribbon. You could have done it yourself in ten seconds with your dressmaking shears.'

'Oh, I daresay you're right!' Aunt Ada knew better than to argue with her husband. It was always wiser to change the subject, so she said:

'Don't forget, on your way back to work this afternoon, you promised to take those old clothes to the

Church Hall for the jumble sale. I promised Mrs Potts she could have them by two o'clock, to leave plenty of time to sort them out for tonight. There are some old shoes in a bag in the bottom of the wardrobe. Better take those, too.'

'Jumble sale!' muttered Uncle Bert disgustedly. 'You'll be wanting a Princess to open *that* next news!'

'Here, try a bit of parkin,' said Aunt Ada soothingly. She cut a very large piece indeed.

5

The sponsored hide-and-seek

Suddenly, a lamp was switched on in a corner of the cellar, and a voice called: 'How did you know where I was?'

It was a girl's voice, and it sounded familiar.

'Who's that?' asked Jake, momentarily blinded by the bright light rising from somewhere near the floor.

'It's Erica Carr!' cried Lenny in amazement.

'It can't be! She's off school with chicken-pox.'

'It *is* me,' said Erica. 'I haven't got chicken-pox, and I'm glad you've come. It wasn't so bad till they left me on my own.'

Erica Carr was the girl who sat next to Lenny in class. Her dad was the richest dad ever to be seen at Cobb Street Primary School. He wore good suits all the time and had a real leather briefcase. Sometimes he brought Erica to school in his Jaguar car. It was certain that Erica would not be allowed to play in an empty house in the Deads all by herself.

'What are you doing here?' Lenny asked her.

'It was supposed to be a sponsored hide-and-seek, for charity. At least, that's what they said last night. You get so much an hour for as long as you stay hidden.'

The boys saw that Erica was installed in some comfort on a

mattress, surrounded by pillows, blankets, comics, refreshments and a reading-lamp.

'I say! It's quite a set-up!' cried Jake admiringly, paying particular attention to a bottle of lemonade and the remains of a custard pie.

'Yes, I thought it was fun at first,' agreed Erica ruefully. 'Especially when they said how much money we were going to make for the new hospital. And last night we had fish and chips for supper and played snakes-and-ladders, and they said I'd have my picture in the papers.'

'*Who* said?'

'This man and woman from Lucci's ice-cream van. They said Mr Lucci was playing as well, hiding somewhere on the other side of town. I just went to buy an ice-cream on my way home from school, and they told me all about it.'

'Erica, you chump! Don't you see, you're not in a sponsored hide-and-seek, you're a hostage? That couple from the ice-cream van are out to get the Princess, and they've captured you first so that if anything goes wrong they'll have something to bargain with.'

'I'm not a chump!' objected Erica. 'I guessed there was something wrong this morning when they said they were going to get the money. You don't collect sponsor-money until it's all over, and I was still supposed to be hiding. They wouldn't have known how much to collect. I'd have gone home, only I fell down the cellar steps when we came in, and I've hurt my ankle. They bandaged it up for me, but I can't walk.'

'Poor old Erica! Never mind, we'll rescue you now, and you'll probably still get your picture in the papers for being a hostage.'

'What about *them*?' asked Jake. 'Don't forget they're chasing us, which is why we ran in here in the first place.'

Even as he spoke, there came a sound of splintering wood, followed by shouts and thuds. Then suddenly there was a terrific crash right over their heads. The foundations shook, there was a din like an exploding bomb, and a great cloud of dust rose up from nowhere, making the children choke and cough.

'What – what's happening?' There were more rumblings and tumblings.

'I think the house has fallen down.'

'Fallen on top of us? You mean we're trapped in here?'

'Looks like it.' Jake had run up the cellar steps and found the doorway completely blocked. 'Mind you, somebody will have heard the din. They're sure to come and rescue us after a bit. You needn't be scared, Erica.'

'I'm not scared. I just wish it *was* a sponsored hide-and-seek. Think how much money we'd be making.'

'That's the stuff, Erica! Tell you what, when we get out of here you can be my conjurer's assistant if you like,' said Lenny generously.

6

The coal-black apparition

The police car, its siren wailing, pulled up with a screech in the middle of the Deads, and a couple of policemen leapt out to survey the damage.

'Collapsed like a house of cards,' said one.

'Well, Fred, we warned the Council, didn't we? We told 'em this lot wasn't safe.'

In the few minutes since the house had fallen, quite a crowd had gathered. It was amazing, thought Fred, where people suddenly appeared from in a crisis. Ten to one there hadn't been a soul in sight five minutes ago.

'Now then, stand back, please! Stand right back! This lot's dangerous!'

Fred turned to his companion. 'Get some more lads down here, George. We want a cordon across both ends of the street. Have to get rid of all these sightseers.'

'There's somebody under there,' a voice cried. 'We were trying to dig him out.'

'It's Mr Lucci,' a woman shouted. 'There's his van, all bashed about. He must have got out of it just when the shop started falling.'

'It's not Mr Lucci, it's a redhead. I saw him just before the wall went down.'

'All right, all right! Let's leave it to the experts. Fire engine's on its way.'

'He might be dead by the time that gets here. You want to do something now.'

'We'll get to him, missus, don't you worry. But if you start jumping about all over that lot you'll only make things worse.'

While all this activity was going on outside, Jake had been mooching thoughtfully round the cellar.

'There's all black grit in this corner,' he said at last.

'That'll be coal-dust,' Lenny explained. He remembered that his grandma had lived in a house like this when she was young. She had often described it to him. All the houses had coal fires then, and the cellar was used to keep the coal in.

Suddenly Lenny had an idea. 'They didn't carry the coal in down all those steps. The coalman used to tip it through a little door at street level.'

Lenny looked up. Somewhere up

there was another little door which might not be blocked with rubble.

'Can you see anything?'

'Put the light out for a minute.'

Jake switched off the light, and Lenny cried: 'There you are! Two little chinks of daylight!'

Lenny climbed up on to an old stone bench and borrowed Jake's knife. He worked the knife blade into one of the chinks of light and followed it round. He discovered a wooden flap with a metal catch on it, but the catch had rusted and he was able to force it outwards with the knife. Dirt and rust fell in on to Lenny's head, but he could smell fresh air.

'Give me a push!'

Jake climbed up beside Lenny on the bench, and hoisted him upwards. At last, Lenny managed to wriggle his head and shoulders into the gap. There was a lot of rubble out there, but he thought he could clear a way through it. He pulled out his arms

and started moving the debris in front of him, stone by stone.

A second police car had just arrived on the scene, bringing two more senior officers. They took over immediately, issuing orders in all directions. Fred was actually on his way to carry out one of those orders at the double when he almost fell over a coal-black apparition which appeared on the ground in front of him. It was Lenny, torn and filthy but triumphant.

Lenny was amazed at the devastation that met his eyes, but he wasn't half as amazed as Fred who had nearly trodden on Lenny's face.

Needless to say, Lenny wasted no time in telling his story. There were two murderers under that rubble, foiled in the act of catching the Princess. There was also their hostage who thought she was on a sponsored hide-and-seek. Once more the tale of the dark blue shopping-bag started, but long before it was finished Fred had concluded that Lenny was suffering from shock.

'Better get him to hospital!'

'Poor lad, he isn't half in a state!'

'Come on, son,' the policeman said kindly, removing his jacket and covering Lenny's shoulders with it. 'Let's get you down to the car.'

Lenny grew frantic with the desperation of wanting to be believed.

'Go and look in that ice-cream van,' he insisted. 'You'll find a conjuring set that belongs to me. . . .'

''Course we will,' Fred replied, humouring him. 'Now, just you get into that seat and relax. We'll have you down at the hospital in no time.'

And that was how Lenny Hargreaves finished up in the Casualty Department of the new hospital, being pushed along a corridor in a wheelchair, just as the Princess's visit was coming to an end.

The royal party was at one end of the corridor, about to turn away to the main entrance and depart, when the Princess spotted Lenny's wheelchair at the other end. The Princess stopped to enquire what had happened to Lenny. A nurse explained about the collapse of the building. Then, ignoring her schedule, the Princess moved sympathetically towards the wheelchair. Lenny felt giddy with relief. At last he could seize a wonderful opportunity to deliver his warning face to face.

'Please, your Royal Highness, there's an ice-cream man out to get you. Somebody's paid him a fortune,

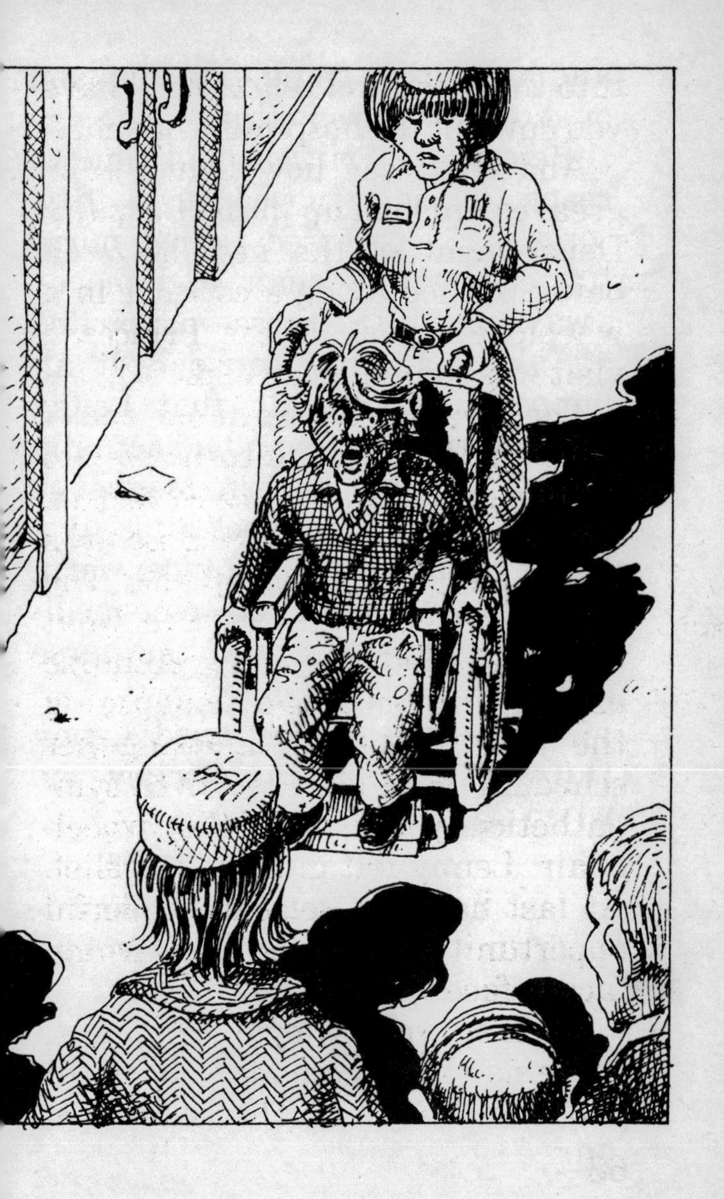

and he's either going to kidnap you or shoot you or something. . . .'

Before the Princess had time to react, officials moved in swiftly, somebody gestured, the nurse turned Lenny's chair and moved away, and the Princess was spirited off along another corridor. It all happened so quickly that Lenny was no longer sure he had actually talked to the Princess. Maybe he was suffering from shock after all.

'We'll put you into a nice, warm bed, dear, and give you some medicine to calm you down,' the nurse said soothingly to Lenny.

'Oh, I give up!' groaned Lenny Hargreaves. 'You'll only believe me when it's too late.'

7

The five-star Princess

The firemen dug carefully through the rubble. They found a man and a woman, both wearing ice-cream jackets, and both with broken legs. They also found a couple of children in the cellar, both of them black as the jack of spades.

So, a little while later, Erica Carr and Jake Allen joined Lenny Hargreaves in the children's ward at the new hospital. Jake was put into the bed next to Lenny, and immediately asked him why they were being treated like dying soldiers.

'They think we're suffering from shock, having hallucinations or something.'

'Yeah,' Jake agreed gloomily. 'I told them about you finding that fiver, and then the bag of money, and they thought I'd dreamed it.'

'Grown-ups are stupid sometimes.'

'Wait till my parents get here,' called Erica from the bed across. 'Everyone will listen to us then.'

It was not long before Mr and Mrs Carr appeared, looking pale and wild. Mrs Carr flung her arms round Erica and burst into tears, while Mr Carr put *his* arms round both of them together, and patted them both on the shoulders. Lenny thought he saw a tear roll down Mr Carr's cheek as well, but he could have been mistaken.

After the touching family reunion, Jake and Lenny defied all

nurses' protests and joined the group round Erica's bed. Then, bit by bit, the story was pieced together.

'They said you had the list of people sponsoring my hide-and-seek,' said Erica to her mother, 'so I thought you'd know where I was.'

'She was really a hostage, of course,' explained Lenny, 'but we rescued her.'

'Well, not a hostage exactly,' said Mr Carr.

'The kidnappers warned us not to tell the police about Erica,' Mrs Carr went on, 'so we rang up the school and said she had chicken-pox.'

'Kidnappers?' echoed Jake.

'Yes, I'm afraid that's what they were. I left the ransom money in the woods, as they told me to. Then I went back later, expecting Erica to be there in exchange, but of course she wasn't. That was a terrible moment,' Mr Carr remembered, 'because the money had gone, yet the kidnappers had not kept their word.'

'Just a minute!' yelled Lenny. 'Did you say *in the woods*? You left the ransom money in the woods? In a dark blue shopping-bag?'

'That's right. The kidnappers took the money. We'll never see that again, but as long as we have Erica safe and sound, that's all that matters.'

'No, they didn't take the money,' cried Lenny, seeing everything clearly at once. 'We took it! It's at the bottom of his Aunt Ada's wardrobe.'

Here he pointed to Jake, who said nobody need worry, the money was safe and sound, because he'd wrapped it up in his Aunt Ada's old brown frock.

'What about the Princess, then?'

'False alarm. We got a bit mixed up,' grinned Jake.

'You mean nobody was going to

shoot her or anything? No wonder they thought we were barmy!'

At that moment the ward sister appeared.

'Come on, you two, back into bed! The doctor's coming to look at you.'

Meanwhile, back at the police station, Constable Barlow picked up the telephone for the umpteenth time and wished it had never been invented. But this time the caller was his wife.

'Is that you, Ben? Oh, thank goodness for that! I've just had the most terrible shock.'

'Look here, Jenny, you can't go ringing me up at work. We've no end of a crisis on here, and I can't sit talking to you. Got to keep the line free for important calls.'

'*This* is an important call, Ben Barlow! I've just had the shock of my life, I tell you! There I was, sorting out jumble at the Church Hall, and what did I find? Only a shopping-bag stuffed full of money, that's all!'

So in the end Jake and Lenny were listened to after all, and their story even found its way into the newspapers. Maybe that was where the Princess saw it. At any rate, she found out what had been going on, and not long afterwards the boys received a parcel with the royal crest on it. The contents included a brand new conjuring outfit and the biggest packet of foreign stamps you ever saw.

'Definitely a five-star Princess,' Lenny said.

THE VANISHING GRAN

Hazel Townson

Having survived their previous adventures in THE GREAT ICE-CREAM CRIME and THE SIEGE OF COBB STREET SCHOOL, Lenny and Jake decide to take a quiet holiday at Gran's only to come across something just as mysterious – for Gran has vanished without trace. Who is the stranger peeping furtively from the deserted house next door; and how is it that the freshly baked rolls in Gran's kitchen are still warm? Lenny, who has brought his conjuring set with him, feels he may be responsible but he couldn't really have made his Gran vanish – could he?

An exciting book for children of seven and above.

Hazel Townson

If you're an eager Beaver reader, perhaps you ought to try some more of our exciting and funny adventures by Hazel Townson. They are available in bookshops or they can be ordered directly from us. Just complete the form below and enclose the right amount of money and the books will be sent to you.

☐	THE BARLEY SUGAR GHOSTS	85p
☐	THE GREAT ICE-CREAM CRIME	£1.25
☐	THE SIEGE OF COBB STREET SCHOOL	95p
☐	THE VANISHING GRAN	£1.25
☐	THE SPECKLED PANIC	£1.25
☐	THE SHRIEKING FACE	£1.25
☐	HAUNTED IVY	£1.25

Postage ______

Total ______

And if you'd like to hear about NEW Hazel Townson titles and more about Beaver Books in general, don't forget to write and ask for our Beaver Bulletin. Just send a stamped, self-addressed envelope to Beaver Books, 62-5 Chandos Place, London WC2N 4NW and we will send you our latest one.

If you would like to order books, please send this form with the money due to:

BEAVER PAPERBACK CASH SALES, PO BOX 11, FALMOUTH, CORNWALL TR10 9EN.

Send a cheque or postal order, and don't forget to include postage at the following rates: UK: 55p for the first book, 22p for the second, 14p for each additional book; BFPO and Eire: 55p for the first book, 22p for the second, 14p for the next seven books and 8p per book thereafter. Overseas: £1.00 for the first book and 25p for each additional book.

NAME..

ADDRESS..

....

Please print clearly